D0189454

Note to parents, carers and teachers

Read it yourself is a series of modern stories, favourite characters and traditional tales written in a simple way for children who are learning to read. The books can be read independently or as part of a guided reading session.

Each book is carefully structured to include many high-frequency words vital for first reading. The sentences on each page are supported closely by pictures to help with understanding, and to offer lively details to talk about.

The books are graded into four levels that progressively introduce wider vocabulary and longer stories as a reader's ability and confidence grows.

Ideas for use

- Begin by looking through the book and talking about the pictures. Has your child heard this story before?

- Help your child with any words he does not know, either by helping him to sound them out or supplying them yourself.

- Developing readers can be concentrating so hard on the words that they sometimes don't fully grasp the meaning of what they're reading. Answering the puzzle questions at the end of the book will help with understanding.

For more information and advice on Read it yourself and book banding, visit www.ladybird.com/readityourself

Book Band 6

Level 2 is ideal for children who have received some reading instruction and can read short, simple sentences with help.

Special features:

Short, simple sentences

Frequent repetition of main story words and phrases

Careful match between story and pictures

Large, clear type

The lift goes up to Daddy Pig's office.

Daddy Pig, Peppa and George all go in.

"This is Mrs Cat," says Daddy Pig.

"Hello, Mrs Cat," says Peppa.

"This is Mr Rabbit," says Daddy Pig.

"Hello, Mr Rabbit," says Peppa.

"Peppa and George are going to see the office," says Daddy Pig.

12

13

14

15

Educational Consultant: Geraldine Taylor
Book Banding Consultant: Kate Ruttle

LADYBIRD BOOKS

UK | USA | Canada | Ireland | Australia
India | New Zealand | South Africa

Ladybird Books is part of the Penguin Random House group of companies
whose addresses can be found at global.penguinrandomhouse.com.

www.penguin.co.uk www.puffin.co.uk www.ladybird.co.uk

Penguin
Random House
UK

Text adapted from 'Daddy Pig's Office', first published by Ladybird Books, 2009
This edition first published by Ladybird Books, 2017
002

This book copyright © ABD Ltd/Ent. One UK Ltd 2017
Adapted by Ellen Philpott

This book is based on the
TV Series 'Peppa Pig'.
'Peppa Pig' is created by
Neville Astley and Mark Baker.
Peppa Pig © Astley Baker Davies Ltd/
Entertainment One UK Ltd 2003.

www.peppapig.com

Printed in China

A CIP catalogue record for this book is
available from the British Library

ISBN: 978-0-241-27966-3

All correspondence to
Ladybird Books
Penguin Random House Children's Books
80 Strand, London WC2R 0RL

MIX
Paper from
responsible sources
FSC® C018179

Daddy Pig's Office

Adaptation by Ellen Philpott
Based on the TV series *Peppa Pig*. *Peppa Pig* is
created by Neville Astley and Mark Baker.

Peppa and George are here to see Daddy Pig's office.

"What do you do at the office?" asks Peppa.

"You will see!" says Daddy Pig.

"This is the intercom," says Daddy Pig.

"Can I press the button?" asks Peppa.

"Yes," says Daddy Pig.

Peppa says hello into
the intercom.

"This is the lift,"
says Daddy Pig.

"Can I press the button?"
asks Peppa.

"Let George have a go this time," says Daddy Pig.

George presses the lift button.

The lift goes up to
Daddy Pig's office.

Daddy Pig, Peppa
and George all go in.

"This is Mrs Cat," says
Daddy Pig.

"Hello, Mrs Cat," says Peppa.

"This is Mr Rabbit,"
says Daddy Pig.

"Hello, Mr Rabbit,"
says Peppa.

"Peppa and George are here to see the office," says Daddy Pig.

"This is what I do at my desk," says Mr Rabbit.

He stamps paper with a stamp.

"Can I have a go?" asks Peppa.

"Yes," says Mr Rabbit.

Stamp, stamp, stamp!

IN

17

"This is what I do at my desk," says Mrs Cat.

She has a computer
and printer.

"Can I have a go?"
asks Peppa.

"No, let George have a go now," says Daddy Pig.

Mrs Cat lifts George up. He has a go on the computer and printer.

Print, print, print!
Peppa and George
are printing with
Mrs Cat's printer.

"Look at all this paper!" says Mrs Cat.

"It's time to go and see my desk," says Daddy Pig.

"Do you have stamps and a computer?" asks Peppa.

"No," says Daddy Pig. "But I have pens!"

"Pens are the best! Can I have a go?" asks Peppa.

Peppa and George like
Daddy Pig's pens.

"This is good!" says Peppa.

Draw, draw, draw!

"Time to go now," says
Daddy Pig.

Daddy Pig's office is good.

"I like Mr Rabbit's job, and I like Mrs Cat's job, but I like your job best, Daddy!" says Peppa.

How much do you remember about the story of Peppa Pig: Daddy Pig's Office? Answer these questions and find out!

- What are Peppa and George going to see?

- Who presses the button for the lift?

- Who does Daddy Pig work with?

- Whose job does Peppa like best?

Look at the pictures and match them to the story words.

Peppa

Mr Rabbit

computer

Mrs Cat

office

Tick the books you've read!

Level 2

- Big Machines
- Camping Trip
- THE ANGRY OWL
- Snoopy's Big Dream
- The Monster Next Door
- On the Farm
- Wild Animals
- School Bus Trip
- The Three Little Pigs
- Little Red Riding Hood
- Nature Trail
- Sports Day
- The Great DRAGON Party
- Emergency Rescue
- Sleeping Beauty
- Superhero Max
- TREEHOUSE RESCUE
- Why Lion ROARRRS!
- The Big Race
- Topsy Tim Go to London
- Playing Football
- Pirate School
- Daddy Pig's Office

Level 3

- Sharks
- Thumbelina
- Aladdin
- YOU won't like this present as much as I DO!
- The Elves and the Shoemaker
- Jack and the Beanstalk
- Harry and the Bucketful of Dinosaurs
- The Jungle Book
- Planet Earth
- Minibeasts
- KUNG FU PANDA SNAKE ATTACK!
- Puss in Boots
- Hansel and Gretel
- Rapunzel